What would you say to someone famous?

✪

"I'd ask what made you pursue acting."
—Elise

"If I met the Kratt Brothers [Chris and Martin Kratt], I'd ask which is their favorite animal and if they have any pets at their homes." —Emmett

"I would say hello, but if he was mean, I'd run back to the car." —Freya

"If I met Kristaps Porzingis, I'd say 'You're my favorite Knick.'" —Owen

"I'd be speechless!" —Lucy

Visit all the states with
Finn and Molly in

MAGIC ON THE MAP!

MAGIC ON THE MAP ②

THE SHOW MUST GO ON

COURTNEY SHEINMEL
& BIANCA TURETSKY

illustrated by STEVIE LEWIS

A STEPPING STONE BOOK™

Random House 🏠 New York

For Eleanor, Beatrice, and John
—C.S.

For Ruby and Ras
—B.T.

Text copyright © 2019 by Courtney Sheinmel and Bianca Turetsky
Cover art and interior illustrations copyright © 2019 by Stevie Lewis

All rights reserved. Published in the United States by Random House Children's Books, a division of Penguin Random House LLC, New York.

Random House and the colophon are registered trademarks and A Stepping Stone Book and the colophon are trademarks of Penguin Random House LLC.

Visit us on the Web!
rhcbooks.com

Educators and librarians, for a variety of teaching tools,
visit us at RHTeachersLibrarians.com

Library of Congress Cataloging-in-Publication Data
Names: Sheinmel, Courtney, author. | Turetsky, Bianca, author. |
Lewis, Stevie, illustrator.
Title: The show must go on / Courtney Sheinmel and Bianca Turetsky;
illustrated by Stevie Lewis.
Description: New York: Random House, [2019] | Series: Magic on the map; #2 |
"A Stepping Stone Book." | Summary: "Twins Finn and Molly Parker are whisked
away in their magical RV to compete in a scavenger hunt in New York City."
—Provided by publisher.
Identifiers: LCCN 2018036688 | ISBN 978-1-63565-169-0 (trade) |
ISBN 978-1-63565-170-6 (lib. bdg.) | ISBN 978-1-63565-717-3 (ebook)
Subjects: | CYAC: Treasure hunt (Game)—Fiction. | Celebrities—Fiction. |
Recreational vehicles—Fiction. | Magic—Fiction. | Brothers and sisters—Fiction. |
Twins—Fiction. | New York (N.Y.)—Fiction.
Classification: LCC PZ7.S54124 Sho 2019 | DDC [Fic]—dc23

Printed in the United States of America
10 9 8 7 6 5 4 3 2 1

This book has been officially leveled by using the F&P Text Level Gradient™
Leveling System.

Contents

Chapter 1

WELCOME BACK

It was late at night on the second day of summer vacation, and Molly Parker couldn't sleep.

The good thing about not being able to sleep on summer vacation is there's nothing you need to wake up for in the morning.

But the bad thing is it gets really boring when you're lying there with the lights turned out.

At least there were some interesting things to think about—like what had happened the day before, on the last day of second grade. Molly and her twin brother, Finn, had come home from school to find a camper in their driveway. It used to belong to someone named Professor Vega. She taught in the astrophysics department at the same college where their dad worked. He had traded his old car with Professor Vega for the camper.

It looked like a regular camper on the outside. It was white with one orange stripe and one yellow stripe, a rounded roof, and three windows on each side.

But inside, it had a PET.

Not an ordinary pet, like a dog or a goldfish. This PET stood for:

Planet

Earth

Transporter.

PET used the information superhighway to travel anywhere in the world within a matter of seconds! Last night they went to Colorado. Molly and Finn spent the whole day there, riding horses, saving a cow, and learning to square dance. But when they returned home, it was only the morning. Their parents were just waking up. They didn't even know the twins had been gone.

Molly wondered if PET would take her and Finn away again tonight. Anything was possible. . . .

Where would they go? And how did the magic work?

There was only one way to find out. Molly

slipped out of bed and put on her fuzzy bunny slippers. She tiptoed so as not to disturb her parents, and wandered outside to the driveway. The camper door was unlocked and opened without a squeak.

"Took you long enough!" Finn said. He

jumped up and tossed his pocket-sized base-ball video game onto the couch. "Are you ready?"

"Hang on, I want to check something," Molly said.

She walked to the bulletin board in the back of the camper, where a map of the world was pinned up, with two pushpins stuck into it. One was in Ohio, where the twins had lived all their lives. The other one was in Colorado. Molly touched the Colorado pin and felt a spark at the tip of her finger. "Whoa," she said.

"Let's go!" Finn said.

Molly raced with her brother to the two big leather seats at the front of the camper. Finn sat down in the driver's seat, just like he had the night before.

Molly took the passenger seat. "I can't

wait to talk to PET again," she said. "I have so many questions."

"Me too," Finn said. "Starting with, where do we get to go this time?"

Molly pressed the POWER button on the TV screen, but the screen stayed dark.

"PET, wake up!" Finn said. "We're back!"

PET was silent.

"C'mon, PET," Finn said. He turned to Molly. "What are we doing wrong?"

"Maybe we need to do all the same things," Molly said. "First, I think you made some *vroom vroom* sounds."

"Okay, *vroom vroom*," said Finn.

"And then . . . ugh. I hate to have to tell you this . . . and then you sang that baseball song you always sing."

"Take me out to the ball game, take me

out with the *crooooooooowd*," Finn sang loudly. Molly put her fingers in her ears. Still, PET did not wake up.

"Maybe the magic was only for one night," Molly said.

"That stinks," Finn said. His video game *whoop*ed from the couch. He got up and headed back to it.

Molly moved to the driver's seat. She

wanted to know how the magic worked. Even more than that, she wanted another adventure. An adventure like the ones she read about in books. She'd read a book called *The Cricket in Times Square*. It was about a cricket who lands in the middle of a bustling New York City subway station. Molly had seen a bunch of crickets at home in Ohio, but she'd never seen a talking cricket, and she'd never seen Times Square. She imagined PET taking her to New York, to the center of Times Square, where she'd meet up with the cricket and his friends.

Except that was just a book. And their magic camper had turned back into a regular old camper. The kind of camper that traveled on roads, not the information superhighway. New York was over five hundred miles away, and Molly got carsick on long rides. She rested her head on the steering wheel and sighed.

"Welcome back," a robotic voice called. Molly whipped her head toward the TV screen. The words "Welcome back" were scrolling across the screen in bright red.

"PET?" Molly whispered.

"That's my name. Don't wear it out!" the camper answered.

Chapter 2

THE NEXT DESTINATION

"PET!" Finn cried, rushing toward the front of the camper. "I knew you'd come back. Molly, give me my seat."

"This time it's Molly's turn to drive," PET said. "Fair is fair."

Finn flopped into the passenger seat. "Well, fine. But remember, next time it's *my* turn."

"Buckle up, kids," PET said. "Molly has chosen our next destination."

"I didn't choose anything!" Molly said.

"Where are we going?" Finn asked.

"That's for me to know, and you to find out," PET said.

The dashboard screen lit up in every color of the rainbow. Molly and Finn grabbed on to their armrests tightly. (Even when you're excited about something, you can still be afraid.) The camper started to hum, then it started to shake. There was a near-blinding flash of white light, and they were off!

Molly squeezed her eyes shut, but she opened them when Finn called out, "Hey! Look!"

A flock of birds with royal-blue and reddish-brown feathers flew by the windshield. "Oh, those are eastern bluebirds," Molly said. "Aren't they beautiful?"

They sailed over a trio of waterfalls, fields of green, and trees. . . .

"I think those are apple trees!" Molly cried.

"Look over there! Is that the ocean?" Finn asked.

"Wow, I think so!"

"Cool!"

But pretty soon the ocean wasn't in sight anymore. All they saw were buildings, and more buildings, and even more buildings. And then the camper landed with a jolt.

Molly still had questions for PET, but she didn't get a chance to ask them. "I'll be back when your work here is done," PET said. With that, the screen went blank. The camper doors swung open. Molly and Finn quickly undid their seat belts and jumped down onto the asphalt.

"Where are we?" Finn asked.

Molly looked around. PET said *she'd* picked the destination, but so far she couldn't tell what it was. They were standing in an alley, in the shadow of tall buildings. In the distance, there were muffled sounds of tires screeching and horns honking. When Molly turned toward the camper again, it had disappeared.

She looked over at Finn. "Uh, Finn," she started. "You're not going to like this." She pointed to something on her brother's shirt.

Finn felt his heart beat a little faster as he looked down. Gone were his plaid pajamas. In their place were blue jeans and a white-and-navy-pinstripe baseball jersey.

"Are you okay?" Molly asked.

"I'm a traitor is what I am," Finn said. He turned around. "What's on my back?"

"The number two," Molly said. "And then over that it says 'Jeter.'"

"Ugh," Finn said. "Jeter. One of the best shortstops in history and a five-time World Series champion."

"That sounds pretty good."

"But he didn't play for any of *my* favorite teams," Finn said. "He played for the Yankees—the New York Yankees."

Finn reached up to the top of his head to feel for what he knew was there—a baseball cap. He almost couldn't bear to look at it, but when he did . . .

Phew!

It was his trusty Little League Moon-walkers cap. He put it back on and folded his arms across his chest, covering up as much of the blue and white as possible. He'd walk around like this all day if he had to.

Molly spun around in delight. "We're in New York!" she cried with glee. "The Big Apple! The City That Never Sleeps! The Empire State!" She paused. "Wait. What am *I* wearing?"

She looked down at her own clothes: black leggings, pink high-tops, and a white T-shirt with the famous logo I ♥ NY.

"I'm going to have to buy some new clothes," Finn said.

"I don't have any money," Molly said. "Do you?"

"I'll figure something out."

"Listen," Molly said sternly. "The magic worked. We're going to have our next big adventure—that's way more important than clothing."

Finn let his arms fall to his sides. "Okay," he said. "Let's figure out what our work is."

Chapter 3

THE MOST FAMOUS KID ON EARTH

The twins ran down the alley toward the sound of traffic. At the end of the street, there was a rush of people passing by. Molly and Finn had never seen so many people in one place in their whole lives. Everyone was walking fast, like they knew exactly where they were headed and they wanted to get there very, *very* quickly.

"Whoa," Finn said. He reached for his

sister's hand, which was not something he could remember ever doing before. "There's gotta be a billion people here."

"Only eight million people live in New York City," Molly said.

Eight million people was still a lot! Besides that, there were stores, hotels, and skyscrapers stretching up practically as high as the eye could see. And there were flashing billboards, and taxicabs speeding by. It was hard to know where to look first, so the twins looked everywhere.

"Look at those signs!" Molly cried. She squeezed Finn's hand tightly.

"Ouch!" he said, pulling his hand away.

"Broadway and Seventh Avenue," she read out loud. "You know what that means?"

"Um . . . we're between Sixth Avenue and Eighth Avenue?"

"We're in TIMES SQUARE!" Molly practically screamed. "I feel like we're at the center of the universe."

"Hey, could that be our work?" Finn asked. He pointed to a sign in the window of a pizza place.

LOOKING FOR WORK?
DELIVERY PERSON WANTED.
BICYCLE REQUIRED.

"Maybe if we work there, we'd get pizza for free," he said.

"I've never heard of eight-year-olds getting hired to be delivery people," Molly said. "And how would we get all the pizzas to their right places without our bikes?"

Finn shrugged. They kept walking. Up ahead, a big circle of people gathered around . . . something. The crowd was blocking the twins from seeing exactly what it was.

But everyone in the circle was looking in the same direction and taking lots of pictures.

"Let's go look," Finn said. He gripped Molly's hand again and ducked into the crowd. When they got to the front, they could hardly believe their eyes.

At least, Molly could hardly believe *her* eyes.

Finn could believe it. He just couldn't understand it. Everyone was flipping out over a kid. People in the crowd were shouting at her.

"Hallie, smile!"

"You're my favorite, Hallie!"

"One more? *PUH-LEASE,* Hallie?"

"Oh. My. Goodness," Molly whispered. "That's Hallie Hampton."

"Was she in your book?" Finn asked.

"Of course not," Molly said. "That book

was about talking animals. It was fiction. That means it was completely made up."

"I know what 'fiction' means," Finn said.

"Hallie Hampton is a real live person," Molly went on. "Look at her!"

"I see her," Finn said. "So what? I'm a real live person, too."

"Hallie Hampton is the star of *Awesome Sauce*, and she may just be the most famous kid on earth!" Molly cried. "I'm going to say hi!"

Molly stepped closer to the one and only Hallie Hampton.

But then something terrible happened. There was a man in a black suit and sunglasses who'd been standing behind Hallie Hampton the whole time. Molly was sure he was a bodyguard. The man leaned down and said something into Hallie's ear. She waved to the crowd and ducked into a stretch limousine. The man slammed the door closed, then gave the roof a couple of hard slaps, as if to say, *All done here. Move 'em out.*

"Oh no!" Molly cried. "Now I'll never get to meet my favorite star."

Chapter 4

HALLIE HAMPTON

Hallie Hampton's limo didn't move. There was a red light and a lot of traffic. The tinted windows were too dark to see inside, and the man in the black suit was blocking the door. Some people in the crowd put down their phones and walked away.

But Molly stepped forward.

"Excuse me," she said.

The man in the black suit didn't seem to hear.

Molly tapped his arm. "Excuse me," she said again. "I ... uh ... I want to meet Hallie Hampton."

"You and every other nine-year-old on the planet," the man said.

Molly was only eight, but that seemed beside the point. "I'm her biggest fan."

"If I had a dollar for every time I heard that," the man grumbled. "Lucky for you, her Broadway debut is tonight at eight o'clock at the Music Box Theatre. They may have a couple more tickets left at the box office."

"How much do they cost?" Molly asked.

"One hundred seventy-five dollars," the man said. "Each."

"We don't have that kind of money," Finn said.

"Well, in that case," the man said, "you can catch Miss Hampton on Thursday nights on TV. Her show—"

"I know," Molly said. "*Awesome Sauce* is on Thursdays at seven-thirty. I've never missed an episode."

Molly felt as if she was about to cry. She couldn't believe there were only a couple of steps and a dark plane of glass separating her and Hallie Hampton. But she might as well have been over five hundred miles away in Ohio.

And then . . .

Something amazing happened.

The limo window rolled halfway down. Hallie Hampton stuck her head out.

"Hey, Tyson. What's the holdup?" she asked.

"Sorry, Hallie. The traffic is terrible."

"Hallie Hampton!" Molly cried.

"Now, look," Tyson said, "Miss Hampton has a schedule—"

Molly ignored him and managed to step

around him. "Please, oh please. I'd do any-thing for an autograph," she said.

"Miss," Tyson said sternly.

But the door was opening!

"Come in," Hallie Hampton said.

"Really?" Molly asked.

"NO!" Finn told his sister. "We can't get into cars with strangers."

"This isn't a stranger," Molly said. "This is *Hallie Hampton*. I know her."

"I don't know about this . . . ," said Finn.

A hole had opened up in the traffic. The limo was blocking the line of cars behind them, and the other drivers started honking their horns.

"If you're going to get in, you have to be quick about it," Hallie Hampton ordered.

Molly dove into the limo, and Finn had no choice but to climb in behind her.

Chapter 5

THE FIRST CLUE

The limo door slammed shut behind them, and the driver took off.

Neither Molly nor Finn had ever been inside a limo before, and it was spectacular! There was a flat-screen TV, a sunroof, and flashing pink neon lights along the walls. Hallie Hampton's newest song, "Summertime Magic," was playing on the speakers.

"Uh . . . ," Molly said. "Uh . . ."

Finn gave his sister a confused look. "I'm Finn Parker," he said. "That's my sister, Molly. She's not usually speechless."

Hallie Hampton grabbed Finn's hand for a shake. Molly wanted to reach out her own hand, but her palm was too sweaty.

Finn nodded toward a line of miniature bottles and snacks. "Hey, is that stuff free?" he asked.

"Take whatever you'd like," Hallie Hampton said. "I won't charge you."

Finn grabbed a chocolate milk. Molly hadn't quite recovered her voice, but she took a bottle of fizzy strawberry cream soda. That's what Hallie Hampton was drinking, and Molly wanted to drink the same thing.

"Thank you," Molly said softly.

"No prob," Hallie Hampton said. "So give me the 4-1-1 on the two of you."

"Is that like 9-1-1?" Finn asked.

Hallie Hampton shook her head. "No. '4-1-1' means give me the deets—the information."

"What do you want to know?" Finn asked.

"Where do you live? How old are you? That kind of stuff," Hallie replied.

"We're from Harvey Falls, Ohio," Finn said. "Next year we'll be in third grade. Oh, and we're twins."

"Bummer," Hallie said. "I thought you were from New York." She pointed at Finn's Yankees jersey. "I need someone who knows this city inside and out. If you're just a tourist, this isn't going to work."

"Wait a second," Molly said. Her voice was getting louder. "Did you just say 'work'?"

"Yeah, I thought you could help me out with something," Hallie said. "But if you're not from here, then we need to say good-bye." She pressed a button on her armrest. The window between the backseat and the front silently rolled down. "Hey, Lou," Hallie called to the driver. "Pull over. These guys are getting out."

"No," Molly said. "I—I may be from Ohio, but I do know a lot about New York. I read a lot."

"It's true," Finn said. "She reads more than I play baseball."

"You're going to have to prove it," Hallie said. She pulled a piece of bright-yellow stationery out of her designer handbag. "*POP Magazine* Scavenger Hunt" was typed in big black letters on the top. Hallie began to read: *"I was born in France, but I've lived in New York City for many years. I have extraordinarily large feet—they're a size 879! Who am I?"*

"You're Hallie Hampton," Finn said. "And your feet aren't that big. I mean, they're bigger than mine, but—"

"I'm not describing myself," Hallie

interrupted. "*My* feet are perfect. This is a clue about someone else in New York."

Molly scrunched up her face in deep concentration. This was a test, and Molly was good at tests.

Hallie tapped her pink nails on the seat. "Speed is very important. If you can't figure it out in the next five sec—"

"The Statue of Liberty!" Molly shouted.

"How do you figure?" Hallie asked.

"No actual person could have shoes that size," Molly explained. "And the statue was a gift from France to the United States, so technically she was *born* in France. Many years ago."

Hallie raised her eyebrows in surprise. "I think you'll do really well with the scavenger hunt. Maybe this will work, after all."

There was that word again—"work"!

"What's a scavenger hunt?" Finn asked.

"It's a kind of game," Hallie said. "You get a clue, and when you solve it, you get the next clue, and on and on."

"I'm happy to solve more clues for you, if you have any," Molly said.

"Correction," Hallie Hampton told her. "You'll solve them on *behalf* of me. You see, *POP Magazine* is having a scavenger hunt for kids. The winner will be photographed by Billie Fischer for the cover of the September issue."

"I just saw you being photographed by practically everyone in Times Square," Finn said. "What's so special about this guy Billie?"

"This *woman*," Hallie Hampton corrected him. "Anyone who's anyone gets to be photographed by Billie Fischer, so obviously *I* need to be. Billie photographed Cleo Feather last month. And now Cleo had the nerve to sign up for this scavenger hunt. She's trying to get a second photo shoot, and I haven't even had one! It's not fair!"

"Who is Cleo Feather?" Finn asked.

"The star of *Catching Up with Cleo*," Molly said.

"I wouldn't say 'star,'" Hallie said. "But it doesn't matter. I need to beat Cleo."

"You and Cleo are the only ones playing this game?" Finn asked.

"No, there are other teams, too," Hallie said. "But I'm really not worried. They're total amateurs."

"That means beginners," Molly told her brother.

"I knew that," Finn muttered.

"I'm too busy to wander all over New York City," Hallie Hampton went on. "Tonight is the opening night of my very first Broadway show. The curtain goes up at eight o'clock, and there's a lot to do before then. The show must go on, you know."

"Oh, I know," Molly said.

"I really should be going over my lines right now so I don't forget any." Hallie lowered her voice dramatically. "You remind me of what is good and possible in this world."

"We do?" Finn asked.

"No," Hallie said. "That's the first line of the whole show. Which just proves how important this part is. Without me, the show can't even begin."

"Whoa," Molly said.

"If you do this hunt for me—and if you win—I'll give you that autograph, *plus* two tickets for tonight's show."

"I'm sorry, but—" Finn started.

"YES!" Molly said loudly. "Tell us where to start."

"Looks like you're starting at the Statue of Liberty," Hallie said. "After that, Lou will take you wherever you need to go. The magazine's rules say you can pick one adult to help you with transportation. Bring this form with you so you can get it stamped at every location."

Molly reached for the form. "Hang on," Hallie said. She pulled out a pen and filled in the lines on the bottom. Under the words "Team Captain," Hallie wrote: Hallie

Hampton. Under "Additional Teammates," she added: Molly Parker and Finn Parker.

They pulled up in front of a big gray building with white columns out front and a row of gold-colored doors. A poster read: "Hallie Hampton in *Happy Trails*." Hallie handed over the scavenger hunt form and scooted out. "Good luck," she called over her shoulder. "Don't let me down."

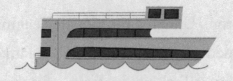

Chapter 6
LADY LIBERTY

"Take us to the Statue of Liberty, Lou," Molly said. "And *quickly*, please!"

"Hold on," Finn said. He turned to his sister. "We can't do this crazy scavenge thing. We need to do *our* work!"

"I think this *is* our work," Molly said. "Hallie kept saying the word 'work.' Didn't you hear her?"

"You just want it to be because she's your favorite star," Finn said.

"Please, Finn," Molly said. "Pretty please with a baseball on top? It's not like any other work has appeared so far—and don't say pizza delivery, because we don't have bicycles."

Finn seemed to be thinking about things.

HONK! went the car behind them.

"Okay, fine," Finn agreed. "Take us to the Statue of Liberty, please."

"Yes, sir," Lou replied.

The limo sped down block after block of shiny marble and glass office buildings. They passed clothing boutiques, coffee shops, and restaurants.

"Whoa," Finn said. "If you took all the streets in Harvey Falls and smooshed them together, there still wouldn't be as much as there is in one New York City block."

"I know," Molly said. "Isn't it wonderful?"

But it was a lot of driving, and Molly started to feel queasy.

"Hey, they have protein bars in every flavor," Finn said. "Want one?"

"Maybe later," Molly said.

Finally, Lou pulled up to the curb and stopped the car. "Here we are," he said. "In record time."

Molly's face had turned a pale shade of green. She jumped out of the limo, and Finn followed behind. They were parked directly in front of a large white-and-red-painted sign that read "Ferry to Liberty Island. Enter here."

"A boat!" Finn cheered.

"A boat," Molly groaned.

Finn and Molly followed the sign to the ticket booth and got in line. When it was their turn, they stepped up to the ticket window.

"Two for Liberty Island, please," Finn said to the girl sitting in the booth.

"You guys under twelve?" she asked. Finn nodded. "That'll be nine bucks each. Eighteen total."

"Is it free for people on a scavenger hunt?" Molly asked.

"It doesn't matter what game you're playing," the girl said. "It costs what it costs."

"Maybe this scavenger hunt isn't our work," Finn said. "We didn't need any money in Colorado."

Reluctantly, Molly and Finn stepped aside so the man in line behind them could approach the ticket window. "Excuse me," he said to the girl. "My wife bought ferry tickets, but I'd already purchased them online. May I return these?"

"Sorry, no returns," the girl said.

"All right, then," the man said. He turned back around. "Hey, anyone need a pair of free tickets?"

"We do!" Molly cried.

"They're all yours," the man said.

"Wow, thanks," Finn said. It seemed too good to be true. The man had just handed over free tickets . . . like magic!

The twins boarded the ferry and found two seats near the railing. Surprisingly, the ride didn't make Molly feel sick. Maybe it was the cool breeze coming off the water. Or maybe it was thinking about all the people who had come from other countries and seen what she was seeing right now—the Statue of Liberty.

The ferry arrived at Liberty Island. Molly and Finn disembarked with the crowd. "Where do you think the next clue will be?" Finn asked.

"I don't know," Molly said. Her eyes scanned Lady Liberty, from the top of her crown to her ginormous size 879 feet. "Maybe inside the statue?"

"Hey, look over there," Finn said.

A man in a bright-yellow *POP Magazine* T-shirt was giving out envelopes to a big group of kids. Molly spotted a dark-haired girl wearing oversized black sunglasses and a red T-shirt with a big black feather on it.

"One at a time!" the man in the yellow T-shirt yelled.

"That's Cleo," Molly said, feeling star-struck again.

"C'mon," Finn said. "Let's get the next clue."

"You two part of the scavenger hunt?" the man asked.

"That's right," Molly said. "I'm Molly Parker, and this is my brother, Finn. We're here on behalf of Hallie Hampton."

Cleo spun around. "Hallie has *you two* doing the scavenger hunt *for* her?" she asked. She lowered her sunglasses to get a better look at Finn and Molly.

"Yep," Finn said.

"Well, please let Hallie know that you ran

into an old friend of hers," Cleo said. "And tell her that I've already picked out my outfit for the photo shoot, so she can forget about having her picture taken by Billie Fischer."

The two kids with Cleo laughed as though Cleo had told the funniest joke. Then they ran off and jumped on the ferry just before the captain pulled up the gangplank. The boat let out a whistle and pulled out of the harbor. Cleo was already in the lead! But this was just the first clue, and Molly was *not* giving up.

Finn and Molly got their form stamped, grabbed an envelope, and raced to catch the next ferry. Soon they were inside the limo once again, staring at the second clue.

Chapter 7

ONE HUNDRED LIGHTNING STRIKES

Molly read the second clue: *"They say lightning never strikes twice, but it strikes me an average of one hundred times a year! That hasn't stopped a giant ape from climbing up my back."*

"No one could survive getting struck by lightning a hundred times," Finn said.

"A person couldn't," Molly agreed.

"Miss Hampton just texted asking for an update," Lou said. "Where are we headed?"

"I'm thinking," Molly said. "It has to be something really tall, because tall things attract lightning."

"Like a giraffe," Finn said.

"I don't think a giraffe could survive that many lightning strikes, either," Molly said.

"Maybe a tree," Finn said.

"A tree would catch on fire," Molly said.

"A skyscraper?" Finn asked.

"That's it! A skyscraper!" Molly cried. "The tallest one would get the most lightning strikes. And I happen to know that the tallest skyscraper in New York is One World Trade Center, also called the Freedom Tower. Lou, can you take us—"

But the limo was moving before she could finish. "Already on my way," Lou said.

It didn't take long to drive to the base of the Freedom Tower. The twins got out of the limo. "Whoa," Finn said. "The tallest sky-scraper in New York looks even higher than I thought it would."

He and Molly crossed a plaza with two enormous pools of water. They weren't the swimming kind of pools. They were more like fountains, but the water went down instead of up.

Finn peeked over the railing. "I've never seen anything like this."

"They're the largest human-made water-falls in all of North America," Molly told him. "The original World Trade Center buildings stood exactly in this spot."

Finn took off his hat and wiped his brow.

"I don't see any of those *POP* people here," he said.

"I bet they're at the top of the Freedom Tower," Molly said. "C'mon."

They rushed to the building. But when they saw that it would cost them twenty-eight dollars each to ride the elevator, Molly's heart sank.

"This city is weird," Finn said. "Elevators don't cost money in Harvey Falls."

Molly was already looking around at the crowd of people in the lobby. She didn't see Cleo Feather's team anywhere. They were probably already at the top, getting the next clue! "Does anyone have any extra tickets?" Molly called. "Anyone?"

No one replied.

"Tickets to go to the top are sold out for today," a uniformed man announced. "If you haven't purchased your tickets already, please come back tomorrow."

"But we have to get up there *today*," Molly told the man.

"Sorry, Miss. Rules are rules. We'll reopen tomorrow at eight a.m."

Molly felt her eyes well up as the man walked away. There was a hard tap on her shoulder. When she turned around, another man was glaring down at her. He was wearing a navy hat and uniform. A badge on his shirtsleeve said NYPD.

"Molly Parker?" the officer asked.

"Yes," Molly squeaked.

"And Finn Parker?" the officer asked.

"That's me," Finn admitted.

"I'm Officer Rodriguez," the officer said. "You two are going to have to come with me."

"Oh no. Did our parents call you?" Molly asked. But wasn't it still the middle of the night back home in Harvey Falls? That's how the magic worked when PET had whisked them off to Colorado. Maybe their mom had woken up to get a drink and discovered their empty beds. *Oh, poor Mom,* thought Molly. *She must be so worried. Dad, too.*

"No, your parents didn't call," Officer Rodriguez said. "But you need to head back to your limo if you want to avoid breaking the law."

"My brother and I didn't break any laws," Molly said. "We actually love laws."

"That's right," Finn agreed. "We never met a law we didn't love."

"Is that so?" Officer Rodriguez asked. "Then you won't mind having your driver move your limo. Now."

"Our driver?" Finn asked, as the officer pushed them out the door of the Freedom Tower. Hallie Hampton's limo was right out front. "Oh, you mean Lou!"

"He's double-parked," Officer Rodriguez said. "You two better get in there and get on your way, or I'll have to issue a ticket." He pulled out a pink pad.

"No!" Molly cried. "We'll get in right now and tell him to move."

The twins jumped into the limo. Finn

told Lou to "step on it," which was something he'd heard in a movie. He turned to look out the back window and breathed a sigh of relief as Officer Rodriguez became smaller and smaller in the distance.

Then Molly pointed out that they still had a problem. "We escaped the police," she said, "but we didn't make it to the top of the building."

"I'll just drive around in circles until you figure out what you want to do next," Lou said. "Hope it's soon. Miss Hampton keeps texting."

Molly's heart was beating fast. She couldn't let Hallie down. But she was afraid she already had.

"Listen," Finn said. "I have an idea. What if the Freedom Tower was the wrong building? There are lots of skyscrapers here that probably get struck by lightning. The clue didn't say it had to be the tallest."

"Yeah," Molly said. "But does that mean we have to go to *all* the tall buildings until we find the right one? We don't have time for that." She paused. "There's got to be something else in that clue to give us the answer."

She pulled it out and read it aloud to Finn. "They say lightning never strikes twice, but it strikes me an average of one hundred times a year! That hasn't stopped a giant ape from climbing up my back."

"Hmm . . . ," Molly said. "A giant ape . . . but I don't think apes live in New York."

"I have a video game where an ape climbs the Umpire State Building," Finn said. "I always wanted to go there to meet all the umpires."

"Wait, Finn. What did you say was the name of the building?"

"The Umpire State Building," he repeated. "An umpire is an official who calls the plays at a baseball game. I think all the umpires must have their headquarters there."

Molly looked at her brother strangely for a moment, and then broke into a huge grin. "Finn, you're a genius!"

"I am?" he asked.

"Yes! Well, sort of. You're wrong about the Umpire State Building, because that's the wrong name. The clue has to be about the *Empire* State Building—it's the second-tallest building in New York City!"

"So it's not the headquarters of all the umpires?" Finn asked.

"I don't think so," Molly said. "But it does have over a hundred floors. I bet it gets hit by lots of lightning."

"Empire State Building, please," the twins called to Lou.

"You got it," Lou said.

Chapter 8

BIRD'S-EYE VIEW

"Look, over there!" Finn exclaimed. He pointed to a woman standing by a hot dog stand, wearing a yellow *POP Magazine* T-shirt.

The twins ran up to her. "Do you have our next clue?" Molly asked, panting.

"No," the woman said. "You have to go to the top for that. But I do have complimentary hot dogs for you if you need some fuel."

"Wow, thanks!" Finn said.

"Yeah, thanks," Molly said. "But look at that line to get to the top. It's gonna take hours."

"That's why I'm here to give you passes to the express elevator." The woman handed over two red tickets. "Go through that revolving door and make a right."

The twins ran through the lobby. They were nearly stopped by a security guard, telling them to get back in line. But when they flashed their passes, he led them to a special elevator. The doors closed, and they shot up.

"Ah, my ears are popping!" Finn said.

"Mine too," Molly said. "I've never been up this high in my life!"

The elevator doors opened, and the first thing the twins saw was . . . a stairwell. After

all that time in the elevator, there were still a few more steps to go! They got to the top of the stairs and walked through a set of double doors. Molly's heart was thumping hard. Standing on the observation deck, she could see all of New York City. She looked over the railing. One hundred and two floors below them, there were cars, buses, cabs, people, and even Lou in Hallie Hampton's limo. Everything looked teeny tiny, like pieces in a game and not real things.

"I hope there's someone from *POP Magazine* up here," Finn said.

"There should be," Molly said. "Let's go find them."

They walked around, looking for someone from the magazine. But they couldn't help noticing other sights, too. "I think that's the Freedom Tower!" Finn cried, pointing. "And the Statue of Liberty!"

"Oh, look over there," Molly said. "All those trees. I bet that's Central Park!"

"Indeed it is," a woman in a yellow shirt said. "You get a bird's-eye view up here."

Wait a second. A *yellow* shirt.

"You're from *POP*! Do you have our next clue?" Molly asked.

"Right here," she said. She presented the twins with a sealed envelope.

Finn held out the form for a stamp. "Has Cleo Feather's team been here already?" he asked.

"I'm not supposed to give out that information," the woman told them. "But I will say that you just missed a group of particularly rude girls. If I were you, I'd hurry."

The twins sprinted for the elevator. There wasn't a second to lose.

The elevator doors had barely closed on the crowded car when they ripped open the envelope. Quickly, Molly glanced around to make sure no other teams were there, then she whispered the clue to Finn.

"I'm a warship parked on a highway since 1982, and so far I haven't gotten any tickets!"

Finn looked at her blankly. Maybe he'd hit a home run on the Umpire State Building (er, *Empire*), but he had no idea what this clue was referring to. It did sound really cool, though.

"A warship parked on a highway for more than thirty years," Molly said to herself. "But ships belong in the sea. It just doesn't make any sense."

"Hey, Dad," a girl in the elevator said. "Look at that. I want an I ♥ NY shirt like the one she's wearing." She nodded toward Molly.

"We got you a T-shirt yesterday," the girl's dad said. "You're wearing it. What do you think, kids?"

"Are you talking to us?" Finn asked.

"I sure am."

"Oh, I like it," Finn said.

Molly looked at the girl's T-shirt—it was navy blue, and under the words "USS *Intrepid*" was a picture of a long gray ship. "Is that by any chance a warship?" she asked.

"It's a warship turned into a military and maritime museum," the man said.

The elevator doors opened. Molly and Finn knew exactly where they had to go. They called goodbye to the girl and her dad, then raced out to Fifth Avenue, where Lou was waiting.

Chapter 9

A CITY ON THE WATER

The *Intrepid* was as big as a building (if a building were lying down on its side), and it wasn't exactly parked on a highway. It was *docked* in the Hudson River, which was right next to the highway.

"You know, I've lived in New York City my whole life, and I've never been here," Lou said. "Would you mind if I come in with you?"

"Well . . ." Molly hesitated.

"Well, what?" Finn asked. "It's a free country. Lou can come in if he wants to. Plus, he's been so nice driving us around all day."

Lou blushed. "It's my job," he said.

"But we *do* appreciate it," Molly said. "Honest, we do. I should have already told you thank you. Thank you, thank you, *thank you*!"

"You're welcome," Lou said.

"It's just," Molly continued, "the rules that Hallie Hampton read were very clear. We're not allowed to have any help from grown-ups, except for transportation."

"What if he comes in to look around but doesn't help us with the next clue?" Finn suggested.

"I think that would be okay," Molly said.

"Great," said Lou. "Ooh! Would you look at that!"

"What?" the twins asked.

"A parking space on Twelfth Avenue. I know the two of you have seen a lot of exciting things today, but trust me when I tell you this free spot is the most exciting one!"

Lou pulled in, and soon the three of them were walking through an entrance marked INTREPID WELCOME CENTER. Just inside was a man in a familiar bright yellow shirt—a *POP Magazine* shirt!

"Hi!" Molly greeted him. "We are Molly and Finn Parker, aka Team Hallie Hampton. Do you have our next clue? Don't worry about this grown-up with us. He's helping us with transportation, but he's *not* helping us figure out anything else."

"Good to know," the man said. "And no, I don't have your next clue. But I do have your tickets and a map, which should help you find it." He handed them over. The map had twists and turns, and a big red "X" in the middle.

"Did Cleo Feather get here already?" Molly asked.

The man nodded. "She picked up her map quite a while ago."

"This place is huge," Finn said, his fingers tracing the different levels and rooms. "It's like a whole city on the water."

Lou's phone began pinging. "It's Miss Hampton. She says to tell you that you're taking too long."

"I know!" Molly cried. "We don't have time to see a whole city. Cleo Feather is *already here*. C'mon!" She called "Thanks" over her shoulder to the man from *POP Magazine* and led her brother and Lou down into one of the tunnels of the warship. There were signs along the walls explaining all sorts of interesting things—that bomber planes had taken off from the *Intrepid*'s flight deck, that there was a giant forty-foot submarine on the ship, and how the forty-thousand-ton ship was able to stay afloat.

They turned a corner. "Would you look at that," Lou said. "A barbershop!"

"Why would anyone come *here* for a haircut?" Molly asked.

"I think it'd be cool to have your hair cut on a warship," Finn said.

"I agree," said Lou. "But I suspect it's not the kind of place that's open to the public. People who lived on warships like this one had to be here for weeks at a time, months even, and during that time, they'd probably need a trim or two."

"If I ever move to New York, I'd like to live here," Finn said. "The rest of the city is so loud and crowded. But this ship has everything I could ever need, and not so many people."

They followed the twists and turns of the map—down one corridor and up another. "I think we go—" Lou started.

"No, don't help us!" Molly said. "We go up those stairs, I think. The 'X' is right at the top."

They raced up the stairs, pushed open a heavy metal door, and then . . .

"Holy guacamole!" Finn said. "We're in an airport! How'd we get to an airport?"

Lou chuckled. "We're still on the ship," he said, patting Finn's head.

The ship deck was a runway, just like an airport. The sides of the runway were lined with all different types of airplanes: spy planes, bomber planes, blue planes, green planes. There was even a space shuttle from NASA! "This is so awesome," Finn said. "Do you think we could go up in one?"

"No!" Molly said. "We need to get our next clue."

"I don't think these are active planes," Lou said. "There aren't any missions being launched off the USS *Intrepid* these days."

"Ah, man," Finn said.

"We have bigger problems," his sister

informed him. "I can't find the person from *POP Magazine*. The map said to come here, but if we can't find the next clue, it doesn't even matter."

"LOUIS!" someone shouted. "LOUIS BRICKMAN, IS THAT YOU?" A man in a blue *Intrepid* shirt stepped out from behind a helicopter, shading his eyes with his hand.

"HOMER HOLBROOK, I DON'T BE-LIEVE IT!" Lou shouted back. "Kids, this is my old pal from flight school, Homer."

"You went to flight school?" Finn asked.

"I did, indeed. I used to give helicopter tours of New York City before Miss Hampton hired me. I tend to keep both feet on the ground these days, but boy, do I miss it."

Just then, the metal door to the roof swung open, and a woman in a yellow *POP Magazine*

shirt stepped out. "Sorry, I had to use the rest-room," she said. "The last team told me you'd dropped out, but I'm glad I double-checked."

"The last team . . . you don't mean Cleo Feather, do you?" Molly asked.

"I can't say," the woman said. "Anyway, you're here now. Since you made it this far, you get a complimentary subscription to *POP*

Magazine for one year, just for participating! Isn't that great?"

Molly gulped. "Does that mean we lost?" she asked.

"Not *yet*," the woman said, stamping the form Finn held out. Then she handed over the next clue.

"Why is this one on blue paper?" Finn asked. "The others were yellow."

"Blue means it's the final clue," she said.

"We're not giving up," Molly said firmly, and she read the clue out loud. "For twenty seasons this was my home. My number may be *two*, but I'm number *one* in the record books." She paused. "Ugh. I have no idea. Maybe we *should* give up."

"No way!" Finn said. "It's the easiest clue yet! I totally know it!"

"You do?"

Finn spun around, revealing the back of his pinstriped baseball jersey.

JETER
2

"Yankee Stadium!" he cried.

"Lou, we've got to get to Yankee Stadium, and fast!" Molly said.

"Wait, aren't you going to tell me what a genius I am?" Finn asked.

Molly yanked his baseball cap down. "Yeah, yeah, you're a genius," she said.

The twins were grinning. But there was bad news. "It's four o'clock," Lou said. "Traffic is going to be at a standstill. I hate to say it, but we may have missed the boat on this one."

"What are you talking about?" Finn asked. "We're *on* the boat right now. We need to get to Yankee Stadium."

"It's an expression," Molly said sadly. "He means it'll take too long to get there."

"I'm sorry," Lou said. "But you're already in last place. I just don't see us getting there in time."

Molly bit her bottom lip. Her eyes began to well up.

"Aw, don't cry, kid. That'll make me cry," Homer said.

"I'm sorry," Molly said. "I just wish the limo could fly over the other cars."

"I can take you in my helicopter," Homer offered.

"We're only allowed one grown-up to help with transportation."

Homer and Lou shared a long look, and then Lou started chuckling. "Hey, Homer," he said, "might I suggest a temporary transportation trade?"

Chapter 10

PREPARE FOR LANDING

Lou was in the pilot seat of a helicopter. *WHOP! WHOP! WHOP!* The propellers started up, and pretty soon they were turning so fast it was all a blur.

"Okay, kids," Homer said, shouting over the noise. "It's time for you to board."

"Oh no!" Finn cried. "My baseball cap!"

The wind from the propellers had lifted it straight off his head. When he ducked back to reach for it, he was blocked by Homer. "No! You must never, ever walk toward the back of a helicopter. Those blades are going three hundred RPM right now."

Finn didn't know what "RPM" meant, but he gathered it was very fast.

"But it's my most prized possession. It's practically—" Finn cut himself off. He knew it sounded silly, but his hat felt like a body part. Being without it made him feel strange and empty.

"Sorry, pal," Homer said, patting Finn's now naked head. "It's time to go."

Finn nodded. At least he'd get to ride in a helicopter. Though, from the looks of it, Molly wasn't excited. Her face had turned as white as a piece of paper. But letting Hallie Hampton down was much more frightening than a helicopter ride. She gritted her teeth and stepped up into her seat.

Helicopter seat belts were different than car seat belts. There were straps that came down over each of their shoulders and more straps that went around their legs, all buckling into a big middle piece. Homer made sure they were secure before he gave the kids enormous earphones to wear.

"Now you're all set," Homer said.

"What?" Finn asked.

Homer lifted one of Finn's earphones and one of Molly's, too. "I'll meet you at the stadium!" he shouted. "It'll take me a bit longer given traffic at this hour, but you're in good hands with Lou. Safe travels!"

He hopped out, and pretty soon they could feel the helicopter lifting off the ground. It was like an elevator—a very fast, very loud elevator, rising straight up in the air. Molly's stomach felt like it had dropped to her sneakers. She was too scared to notice the popping in her ears, and Finn was too excited. They moved forward, flying over the Hudson River. Out the window, New York City looked like a Lego set.

Finn was the first to spot Yankee Stadium. He could see the green grass of the field, the brown dirt of the baselines, and the giant white Yankees logo painted behind home plate. Molly was straining to see what was below, too. She thought she saw some people dressed in yellow. And outside the stadium, she was pretty sure she saw a group of kids in red shirts getting out of a white SUV and running toward the entrance.

"It must be the Feathers!" she said.

"What?" Finn asked.

"THE FEATHERS!" she screeched. But he couldn't hear her. She could hardly hear herself.

Lou spoke to them through his headset microphone. "Prepare for landing, and hold on tight."

Molly gripped her seat as the helicopter started its descent. It was like going straight down in an elevator, except way bumpier. They landed far out in center field. Lou turned off the engines, and the twins took off their headsets and tried to undo their complicated seat belts.

Molly banged hers with the heel of her hand. "I can't get it loose!"

"Hang on," Lou said. "Those things are locked pretty tight for safety reasons."

He came around and snapped them open in a jiffy. "C'mon," Molly called to her brother.

There was a cluster of bright yellow by home plate—people in yellow shirts holding yellow balloons. That could only mean one thing: they were *POP Magazine* people ready to award the winner.

The twins ran as fast as they could. In the back of Finn's head, he imagined himself running the bases on this field, the crowd going wild. "PARKER! PARKER! PARKER!" they'd shout. He could hear the commentators over the loudspeaker: "It looks like Finn Parker is going for another home run. Once again, it's Parker saving the day!"

But that was make-believe. In real life, there was another person shouting: Cleo Feather. "You guys and your friend Hallie Hampton are *going down*!" she said.

THWAP!

"You see— *DOWN!*" Cleo said.

"Molly!" Finn cried.

His sister was facedown in the grass, and beside them was the passing sound of laughter as Cleo and her friends ran by.

Finn shook his fist. "Why, you—" he screamed at Cleo's back.

"No," Molly said. "There's no time to be mad, Finn. You need to run. *RUN!*"

Molly was right. The Feathers were way ahead now. But Finn pressed forward. It was like his Moonwalkers coach always said: "Keep your eye on the prize—home plate."

Finn kept his eyes on home plate and began to sprint. He caught up with Cleo Feather, but try as he might, he couldn't overtake her. She was matching him stride for stride. When Finn got close enough, he dove for home plate. Cleo skidded to a stop behind him.

A man in a yellow *POP Magazine* shirt reached down and helped Finn to his feet. "That play could get you signed to the Yankees," he said.

Finn was nearly breathless, but he managed to pant out, "Thanks." He bent forward, resting his hands on his knees, waiting for the air to come back into his lungs. He could hear Cleo complaining that it wasn't fair—Finn and Molly had taken a helicopter.

"The helicopter was fair play," the man responded.

"I want to talk to whoever is in charge," Cleo demanded.

"I'm in charge," a woman replied.

Finn looked up to see a woman with a short spiked hairstyle and a giant camera hanging around her neck. He took a deep breath. "You're Billie Fischer, aren't you?"

"The one and only."

"Wow, it's really nice to meet you. Your scavenger hunt was great—hard, but great. And we got to go to amazing places."

"I've taken my favorite photos at those places," Billie said. "That's why I picked them for this hunt."

"I can't believe we won," Finn told her.

"I'll just need to see your form to make it official."

Finn pulled out the team form that was crumpled in the back pocket of his jeans and handed it to Billie.

"Ah," Billie said as she read. "This is very interesting."

"What?"

"It seems that you're not the winner, after all."

"What?" Finn exclaimed. "Of course I am. I mean, we are. Our team got here first."

Billie shook her head. "Your *team* did not," she said. "It is just you here at the finish line. There are two other team members listed on this form, and—"

"I'm here!" Molly cried, hobbling forward. "Molly Parker."

"You are still missing your team captain," Billie Fischer said, glancing at the form. "Hallie Hampton. So that means—"

"*We* win," Cleo Feather supplied. She turned to the twins. "Tell Hallie we *really* missed her today. Not!"

"I lost my Moonwalkers hat for nothing," Finn said, kicking the dirt.

Molly kicked the ground, too. Her ankle throbbed. Having a twisted ankle would've been worth it if they'd won, but now . . .

"Not so fast," Billie said to Cleo. "I saw you trip your competitor here. That's cheating, which is against the rules."

"I did not," Cleo said. "It's just that she's a total klutz."

"Pictures don't lie," Billie said. "Unfortunately, people sometimes do." She took the camera off her neck and scrolled through the screen on the back. There was Cleo, foot out to trip Molly. "I imagine that's not the photo shoot you had in mind."

Finn couldn't help smiling.

"So . . . ," Molly said. "We won, after all?"

"No. Rules are rules," the man from *POP Magazine* said. "And we are still waiting for team number three."

"Those losers?" Cleo asked in disbelief.

"I'd say they are the winners," Billie Fischer told them.

"You tried your best, kids," Lou told the twins. "In my book, that counts as good work."

Homer walked up to the group, and he and Lou exchanged keys—limo keys for helicopter keys.

"We've got to head back to meet Miss Hampton at the theater before the curtain goes up," Lou said.

"You left something important at the *Intrepid*." Homer handed Finn his Moon-walkers hat.

Finn put it on his head and felt instantly better—more like himself. Plus, Lou had said the word "work." Maybe he and Molly had done what they were sent to New York to do, and PET would be waiting by the theater. Finn felt sad for Molly that they'd miss the show and getting Hallie's autograph.

But it had been a long day, and he was ready to go home.

Chapter 11

BREAK A LEG

Lou texted Hallie with a last update to say their team had been disqualified. Hallie might refuse to see them. They wouldn't get to say goodbye, but maybe that was better.

Lou pulled up in front of the Music Box Theatre, and the twins climbed out of the limo. They didn't see the camper anywhere. Instead, a man with a clipboard was holding open the heavy theater door. "Are you Molly

and Finn Parker?" he asked. The twins nodded. "Miss Hampton is expecting you."

Molly felt a knot in her stomach, like she
was walking into a test that she hadn't pre-
pared for. Although that had never happened
before.

"Miss Hampton is in her dressing room,"
the man said. "We've got to move quickly. It's
almost curtain time."

"We can come back later. We don't want to
disturb her on opening night," Molly offered.

"She's waiting for you. Let's move." He led
them to a door with a big gold star on it that
read HALLIE HAMPTON. Molly wanted more
time to prepare herself, but the man rapped
three times on the door, and it swung open.
There was Hallie Hampton wearing a glit-
tery costume and a feather boa.

"Well, well, well," she said, her arms folded across her chest. "Seems I trusted the wrong kids with the most important task."

"We're so sorry," Molly said.

"Speak for yourself," Finn said. "I'm not sorry—and even if Molly is, she shouldn't be. We worked so hard for you today. We traveled this city from the bottom to the top, and we *won*!"

"You won?" Hallie asked. "But Lou said—"

"Well, we would've won," Finn said. "It's *your* fault that we didn't. You wrote your name down as team captain."

"I *was* the team captain!" Hallie insisted. "I'm the one who was invited to join the scavenger hunt. You wouldn't have even known about it if it weren't for me."

"If you knew so much about the hunt,

then you should've known that all team members needed to be at the finish line," Finn said.

"Five minutes to curtain!" the man told Hallie. He turned to the twins. "You two better take your seats."

"Oh, they don't have any seats," Hallie said. "They're leaving now."

"Break a leg," Molly called to Hallie's back. Hallie didn't answer.

"That was kind of mean," Finn said.

"It means good luck," Molly explained.

"Oh," Finn said. "Well, she doesn't really deserve luck. She's not very nice."

"No, she's not," Molly agreed miserably. It was sad to meet her favorite star—the person she thought that if she ever did meet, they'd surely be best friends—only to find out that they didn't like each other. "I guess we should just go."

But getting out of the Music Box Theatre was easier said than done. They didn't have a map, like they'd had on the *Intrepid*. It was hard to remember the order of the turns back to the door. "I think we're going the wrong way," Finn said.

"Which way should we go?" Molly asked.

"I don't know," Finn admitted.

They kept walking. The corridors were dark and narrow, but Molly saw light up ahead. When they got closer, they couldn't believe their eyes.

It wasn't a door. It was the stage. Hallie Hampton was right in front of them, illuminated by a spotlight. Molly sucked in her breath and grabbed Finn. Together, they made

sure to stay out of sight of the audience—and
of Hallie Hampton.

But they couldn't help but watch. Hallie
was just . . . standing there. It was almost as if
she was frozen in place. "This is kind of a boring show," Finn whispered.

"*Shhh,*" Molly said. "I'm sure she'll say the
first line any second now."

Hallie was quiet.

"Any second," Molly repeated.

Hallie didn't say a word. There were murmurings in the audience. "Cat got your tongue?" someone in the audience said. There was a snicker throughout the crowd.

Hallie looked toward the twins. Molly was pretty sure she couldn't see them, because they were hidden by the darkness. But she could probably *hear* them.

Molly felt the same twitchy feeling she sometimes had in school, when the teacher asked a question she knew the answer to. She couldn't help herself from blurting it out.

"You remind me of what is good and possible in this world," Molly said. She tried to be quiet. But it was loud enough for Hallie to hear, and she whipped her head toward Molly.

Molly gulped, afraid that she had ruined everything again. But Hallie just winked. "You remind me of what is good and possible in this world," Hallie repeated, and then she kept going.

Chapter 12

OPENING NIGHT

It was the best play Molly and Finn had ever seen. The audience gave Hallie a standing ovation that went on for at least ten minutes. People kept throwing flowers onto the stage. Hallie took a deep bow and ran backstage, where Molly and Finn were waiting.

Molly wasn't sure what to expect when Hallie ran up. Would she still be mad about the scavenger hunt? Would she be mad Molly said the first line?

Hallie threw her arms around Molly. "Thank you," she said. "Thank you *so much*! You too, Finn."

"I didn't do anything," Finn said.

"You were here for moral support," Hallie insisted. "It meant a lot. I know I've been awful to you today."

"No, you weren't," Molly said, at the same time that Finn said, "Yeah, you were."

"I was really nervous about opening night," Hallie said. "I took it out on you guys. Please forgive me."

"We do," Molly said, and Finn nodded.

"Here, take these." Hallie handed over a bouquet of pink and purple roses.

"Wait. I want to give you something, too. I made it," Molly said. She tugged at the friendship bracelet on her wrist. She felt herself blushing. Yesterday, when they'd traveled to Colorado, she'd given another friendship bracelet to her new friend Ella. She wanted to give *this* one to Hallie, but why would someone as famous as Hallie want to be her friend?

"I love it!" Hallie said.

"I know you probably have a ton of

friends and a whole closet full of friendship bracelets."

"I have a lot of bracelets," Hallie said. "But no one's ever given me a *friendship* bracelet before. This is really cool."

"Hallie Hampton, you are a genius," a raspy voice shouted.

"Billie Fischer!" all three kids exclaimed at once. She was wearing a dress, and she still had her camera hanging around her neck.

"I'm a big fan of yours," Hallie Hampton told her.

"Why, thank you," Billie replied. "I'm a big fan of yours now, too."

"Would you mind . . . ," Hallie said. "I mean, I know we didn't win the scavenger hunt, but could you take a picture of me and my friends?"

"It would be my pleasure," Billie said. Hallie put her arm around Molly's and Finn's shoulders. "Smile!"

Afterward, Billie said her goodbyes and promised to send the photo to Hallie as soon as possible.

"I'll always remember you guys now, because I'll have this picture, plus the bracelet," Hallie told the twins. "Not that I could ever forget you. Thanks for rescuing me tonight. And thanks for all your hard work."

Molly and Finn caught each other's eyes. Hallie had said the magic word: "work." They knew what was coming, and sure enough, seconds later, they heard a familiar honking outside.

"Sorry, but we've got to go," Molly said.

Hallie Hampton gave them each a hug

goodbye, and then she was swept away into the crowd of fans. Molly and Finn made a run for the door. The camper was parked right outside the theater, and PET's screen was already lit up when the twins climbed in. "Buckle up, kids," it said. "Next stop: Harvey Falls!"

The instant they clicked their seat belts, the camper took off. They flew over buildings, waterfalls, and fields of green. Then they stopped with a jolt. "My work here is done," PET said.

"Wait, PET," Molly said. "Don't go yet! I have questions for you: How do you work? Is it magic? Is it science? Did Professor Vega make you?"

"Sorry. Your access is denied," PET said, and the screen went dark.

"C'mon," Finn said. "Let's get breakfast."

"Okay," Molly said.

But before they stepped outside, Molly walked to the world map at the back of the camper and pushed a red pin into New York City. "There," she said, then followed her brother out to 24 Birchwood Drive.

New York State Facts

✪ The New York state tree is the sugar maple. The state flower is the rose, and the state bird is the eastern bluebird.

✪ The New York state flag looks like this:

✪ Niagara Falls is the name for three waterfalls that straddle the international border between the Canadian province of Ontario and the American state of New York. Bridal Veil Falls is the smallest of the three waterfalls, and Horseshoe Falls is the largest.

✪ Albany is the state capital.

✪ New York is bordered by five states (Vermont, Massachusetts, Connecticut, New Jersey, and

Pennsylvania), two Canadian provinces (Ontario and Québec), two of the Great Lakes (Lake Erie and Lake Ontario), and the Atlantic Ocean.

✪ The Statue of Liberty was a gift to the United States from France in 1885, and it has welcomed over twelve million immigrants entering the country through New York Harbor and Ellis Island. Not only are her feet a size 879, but her nose is over four feet long!

✪ There are over eight million people living in the five boroughs of New York City—Manhattan, Brooklyn, Queens, the Bronx, and Staten Island. Finn and Molly went to two boroughs, Manhattan and the Bronx.

✪ The Empire State Building is 103 stories high. Finished in 1931, it was the tallest building in the world. In 1972, the original World Trade Center buildings, aka the Twin Towers, became the two tallest buildings in the world. The Twin Towers were destroyed in a terrorist attack on September 11, 2001. Today, One World Trade, also known as the Freedom Tower, is the tallest building in the Western Hemisphere and the sixth-tallest building in the world.

○ The *Intrepid* is 912 feet long by 192 feet wide, which is equal to about three football fields.

PET's favorite New York fact:

○ The Empire State Building has been featured in more than 250 movies! The most famous one is probably *King Kong*. In it, a giant ape (named King Kong) climbed the skyscraper.

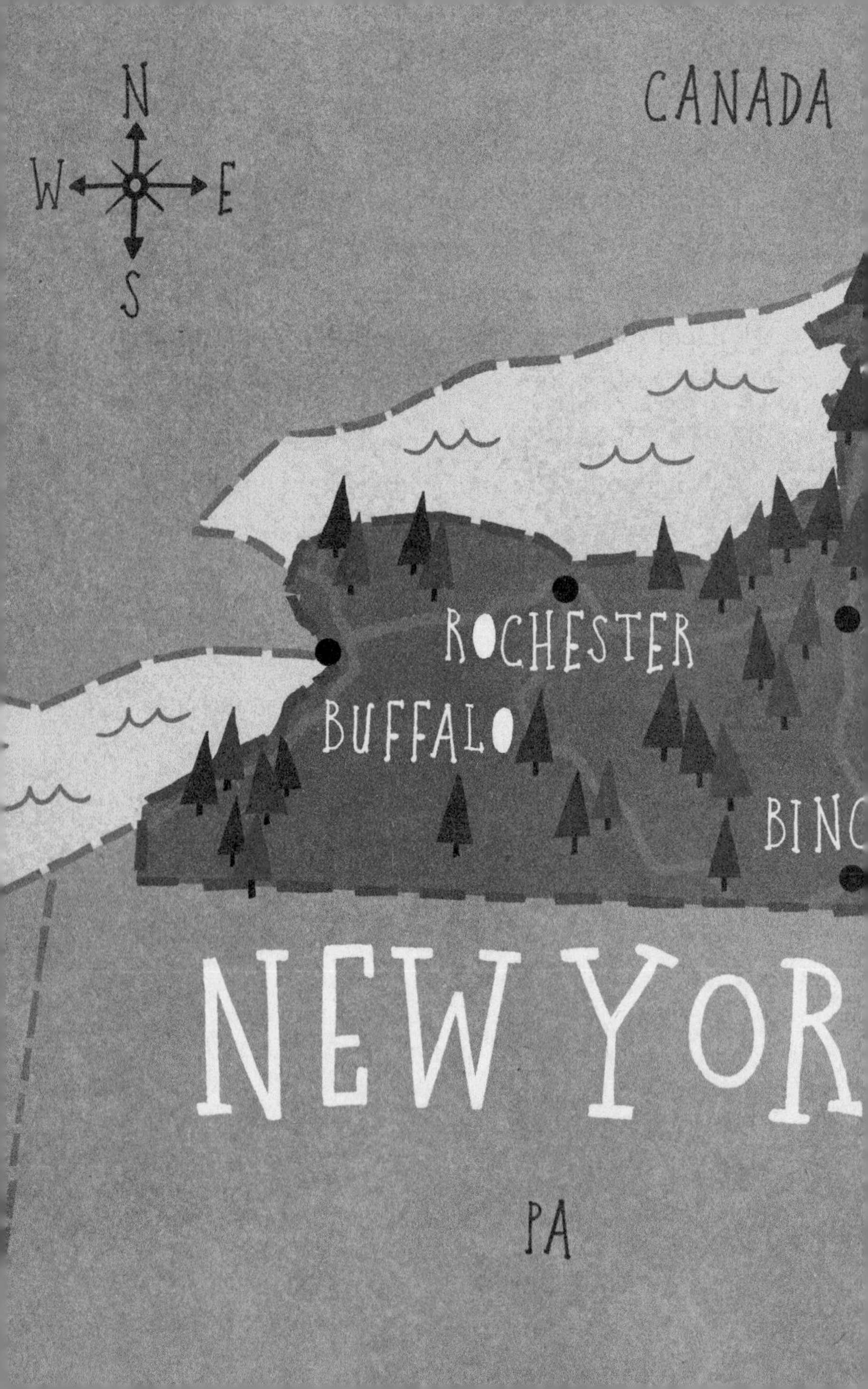
N
W
E
S
CANADA
ROCHESTER
BUFFALO
BING
NEW YOR
PA

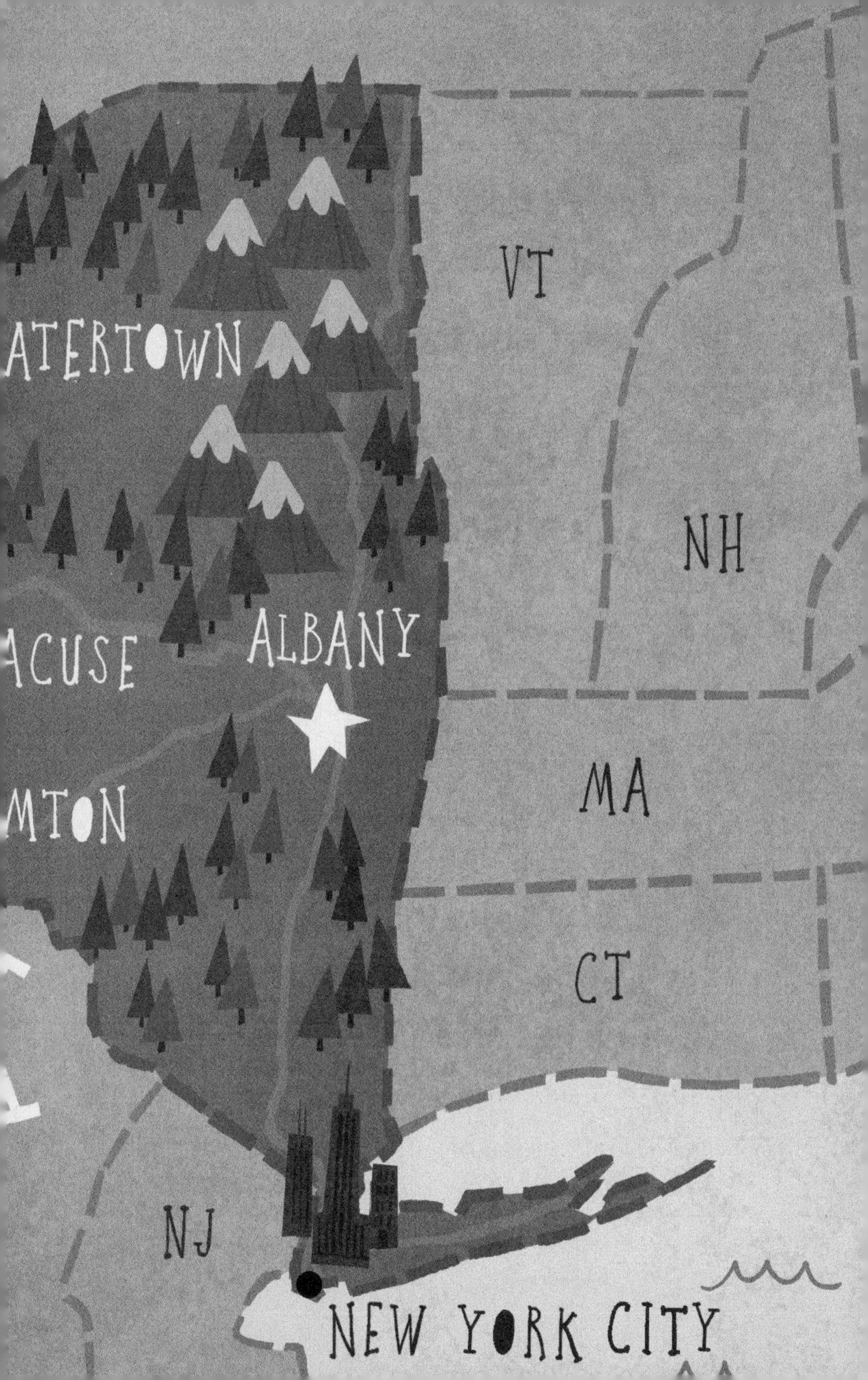
ATERTOWN
VT
NH
ALBANY
ACUSE
MA
MTON
CT
NJ
NEW YORK CITY

Finn and Molly's work here is done,
but the adventures continue!

Don't miss their next mission!

MAGIC ON THE MAP ③

TEXAS TREASURE!

"Whew, it's hot," Molly said. "Even hotter than Ohio. Good thing I'm in this sundress. I love the cowboy boots, too."

"Oh no. Oh no. Oh no," Finn said. "Do *not* tell me I'm wearing an Astros jersey! I can't do that to the Reds!"

He looked down to see what he was wearing: a plaid button-down shirt, jeans, and a wide belt with a big silver buckle.

"Oh, phew," he said. "Now our only problem is finding the stadium. Let's ask someone . . . maybe that guy."

He pointed to a man in a brown jacket and a matching wide-brimmed hat.

"Why would someone be wearing a jacket in this weather?" Molly asked.

Finn shrugged. "It doesn't matter. We're asking him for directions, not fashion advice."

Before Finn could step forward to talk to him, the man threw up his arms and shouted, "What are we going to do? General Santa Anna and his men are coming!"

"Santa Anna . . . Santa Anna," Molly said. "That name is kind of familiar."

"Not to me," Finn said. "But from the sound of it, I doubt it's anyone I'd want to meet."

Another man strode across the courtyard.

He was carrying a crate under his arm and wearing a fur hat with a striped tail hanging off the back. Maybe he was Santa Anna! Finn and Molly scooted back and hid behind a wall, just in case.

Other people came forward and gathered around the man in a semicircle.

"Is that who I think it is?" a woman asked loudly.

"I think so," a man answered.

"I heard he killed a hundred bears in one season," the woman said.

"I heard he can ride a streak of lightning," the man replied.

"Oh my goodness," Molly whispered to Finn. "That man with the crate—I think he's Davy Crockett!"

Can you guess where
Finn and Molly are?

Travel with Finn and Molly in the

 books!

Have you read them all?